D0403915

CLEMENTINE ROSE

ROSE

and the Farm Fiasco

Books by Jacqueline Harvey

Clementine Rose and the Surprise Visitor
Clementine Rose and the Pet Day Disaster
Clementine Rose and the Perfect Present

Alice-Miranda at School
Alice-Miranda on Holiday
Alice-Miranda Takes the Lead
Alice-Miranda at Sea
Alice-Miranda in New York
Alice-Miranda Shows the Way
Alice-Miranda in Paris

CLEMENTINE ROSE

and the Farm Fiasco

Jacqueline Harvey

RANDOM HOUSE AUSTRALIA

A Random House book
Published by Random House Australia Pty Ltd
Level 3, 100 Pacific Highway, North Sydney NSW 2060
www.randomhouse.com.au

First published by Random House Australia in 2013

Copyright © Jacqueline Harvey 2013

The moral right of the author has been asserted.

All rights reserved. No part of this book may be reproduced or transmitted
by any person or entity, including internet search engines or retailers,
in any form or by any means, electronic or mechanical, including
photocopying (except under the statutory exceptions provisions of
the Australian *Copyright Act 1968*), recording, scanning or by any
information storage and retrieval system without the prior written
permission of Random House Australia.

Addresses for companies within the Random House Group can be found at
www.randomhouse.com.au/offices

National Library of Australia
Cataloguing-in-Publication Entry

Author: Harvey, Jacqueline
Title: Clementine Rose and the farm fiasco/Jacqueline Harvey
ISBN: 978 1 74275 547 2 (pbk.)
Series: Harvey, Jacqueline. Clementine Rose; 4
Target audience: For primary school age
Subjects: Girls – Juvenile fiction
          School field trips – Juvenile fiction
          Farms – Juvenile fiction
Dewey number: A823.4

Cover and internal illustrations by J.Yi
Cover design by Leanne Beattie
Internal design by Midland Typesetters
Typeset in ITC Century 12.5/19 by Midland Typesetters, Australia
Printed in Australia by Griffin Press, an accredited ISO AS/NZS
14001:2004 Environmental Management System printer

Random House Australia uses papers that are natural, renewable and
recyclable products and made from wood grown in sustainable forests.
The logging and manufacturing processes are expected to conform to the
environmental regulations of the country of origin.

For Darcy, Flynn and Eden,
and for Ian, the best 'manager'
anyone could ever wish for.

CRACK!

Clementine Rose gripped her pencil and stared at the page. Mrs Bottomley said that they should try to spell a word before asking for help. Clementine thought for a moment. Then, as neatly as she could, she wrote the letters *h-a-t-c-h*.

Mrs Bottomley was walking around the room inspecting everyone's work. She stopped beside Clementine's desk and squinted through her glasses.

'Let me see what you've got there, Clementine. *The egg is going to hatch.* Where did you copy that from?'

Clementine shook her head. 'I didn't. I wrote it myself.'

Mrs Bottomley's forehead puckered. 'Come now, Clementine. Perhaps Astrid might have helped you?' She smiled at the girl sitting behind Clemmie.

Clementine looked up at her teacher. 'No, Mrs Bottomley. I sounded it out by myself.'

'If you say so,' the teacher replied, pursing her lips.

Clementine frowned. She wondered why Mrs Bottomley didn't believe her. 'May I go and see if anything's happening?' she asked.

'Happening?' Mrs Bottomley repeated. 'Where?'

Clementine pointed. 'Over there.' Mrs Bottomley wasn't very good at remembering things sometimes.

'I think you should draw a picture first, and then you can have a look – although I don't imagine anything will have changed in the last few minutes.'

Clementine began to draw her illustration at the bottom of the page. She was trying to imagine what the chick would look like. She thought it would be fluffy and yellow, like the picture of a chick that was stuck up on the back wall.

Mrs Bottomley disappeared into the storeroom. Clementine stood up and walked towards the incubator. It had been set up on a table at the back of the room by Poppy's father, Mr Bauer. It had glass sides and glaring lamps, and eight creamy eggs sitting inside.

'Come on, little chickens,' she whispered. 'Please come out soon.'

The eggs sat perfectly still.

Clementine hadn't noticed Angus standing behind her.

'I'm going to eat those eggs for breakfast tomorrow,' he said.

Clementine spun around. 'No, you can't! They're not breakfast eggs, they're chick eggs.'

'They're boring eggs,' Angus sneered. 'They don't do anything.'

While Angus babbled on about his mother making an omelette, something caught Clementine's attention.

She put her finger to her lips. 'Shh! Look!'

'There's nothing hap–' The boy stopped suddenly. 'It just moved.'

Clementine and Angus watched as one of the little eggs rocked from side to side. They peered closer and then looked at each other and smiled.

'Something's coming out!' Angus exclaimed.

'Angus, Clementine, neither of you have finished your work,' said Mrs Bottomley as she emerged from the storeroom. 'I said that you could look at the eggs once your drawings were done.'

'Mrs Bottomley,' Clementine called. 'One of the eggs is moving.'

The whole class stopped what they were doing and looked around.

'Cool,' said Joshua. He slid out of his seat and raced over.

'Joshua Tribble, go back to your desk,' Mrs Bottomley directed.

Clementine and Angus hadn't moved. Their eyes were glued to the glass case.

'There's a beak, there's a beak!' Clementine shouted.

The rest of the class ran towards the incubator.

'Sit down at once.' Mrs Bottomley's voice boomed, but she didn't stand a chance against a mob of excited five-year-olds.

The head teacher, Miss Critchley, happened to be passing the classroom and looked in to see the children rushing around like a swarm of bees.

'What's going on in here?' she asked cheerfully as she strode into the room.

'Children, sit down!' Mrs Bottomley demanded.

'Miss Critchley, there's a beak,' Clementine shouted above the din.

'All right, everyone, settle down.' Miss Critchley's voice was like honey. The children stopped their shouting at once. 'You don't want to frighten the chick, do you? Gather around. If you're in the front, please kneel down so the people behind you can see.'

Mrs Bottomley harrumphed loudly and moved in behind Joshua.

The whole class was transfixed as the little egg shook and the tip of a beak broke through again.

'It needs my dad's saw,' Joshua said.

'I think it's doing a wonderful job with its beak,' said Miss Critchley, smiling. The little hole was spreading out to become a line around the middle of the egg.

'As if a chicken would have a saw inside an egg. That's stupid,' said Angus.

Joshua poked out his tongue. '*You're* stu–'

Miss Critchley interrupted the lads. 'There'll be no name-calling, thank you, boys. Let's just see what happens.'

The children watched as the chick made

more cracks in the shell. They oohed and aahed as the tiny creature began to break free.

'This is boring,' Joshua complained. 'How long does it take to get out of an egg?'

'You could sit down and do your work,' Mrs Bottomley suggested.

'That's more boring,' said Joshua.

There was a loud gasp as the egg finally broke in two and a wet chick wobbled to its feet.

'It's brown,' Angus said, clearly surprised.

'Like Mrs Bottomley.' Joshua laughed and turned around to look at his teacher. She was dressed in her usual uniform of brown shoes, brown stockings and a brown suit.

Clementine bit back a smile. She couldn't remember seeing her teacher wear any other colour.

Mrs Bottomley simply raised her eyebrows and the grin slid from Joshua's face.

'Do you think the other chicks will hatch soon?' Clementine asked.

Miss Critchley nodded. 'Yes, they shouldn't be too far behind.'

'Will we be able to hold them?' Sophie asked.

'You have to be careful,' said Poppy, 'because they can get cold.'

Everyone knew that Poppy was an authority on animals, as she lived on a farm.

'I'm gonna hold it first,' Angus declared. 'I saw it first.'

Astrid stared at the boy. 'Clemmie saw it first. She should have first hold.'

'Yes, I think that sounds fair,' said Miss Critchley. She winked at Clementine.

'Angus can go first if he wants to,' Clementine said.

The boy shrugged. 'It's okay, you can go.'

Clementine smiled. Sometimes it was hard to believe that Angus was the same boy who had been so horrible to her at the start of the year.

'I think we should give the chick a little while to get used to its surroundings,' said Miss Critchley. 'Why don't you all head back to your desks and I'll come around and have a look at your work.'

9

The children sped to their seats, eager to show their writing to the head teacher.

'Mrs Bottomley, do you have any stickers?' Miss Critchley asked.

Ethel Bottomley had a very large collection of stickers in the bottom of her desk drawer, but she used them sparingly.

'I suppose you could have these.' She pulled out a flat page of silver stars. The corners were slightly dog-eared.

Miss Critchley walked through the room admiring the children's work and sprinkling each page with stars, much to Mrs Bottomley's displeasure.

When she reached Clementine, Miss Critchley congratulated her on her efforts and suggested they sneak over to the incubator to see how the chick was getting on.

Clementine's eyes widened as she looked at the little bird. 'It's fluffy!'

'And I think it's about to get a new friend.' Miss Critchley pointed at another egg that was rocking gently. 'Would you like to hold the chick now?'

Clementine nodded. She'd never held a newly hatched chick before.

Miss Critchley reached in and gently picked up the baby. She told Clementine to hold her hands open and then placed the chick inside.

'It's so soft.' Clementine's smile was wide and her eyes sparkled.

'What do you think we should call him or her?' Miss Critchley asked.

Clementine thought hard. 'I think it's a girl. Her feathers feel like the velvet material Mrs Mogg used to make me a winter dress. Could we call her Velvet?'

'I think that's perfect, Clemmie,' Miss Critchley declared. 'Hello Velvet.'

B y the end of the school day, three more chicks had hatched. Velvet had been joined by Lemonade, named by Angus, Henny Penny, named by Astrid, and Joshua, who'd been named by the boy himself.

Clementine wondered if all eight chicks would be there when they arrived for school the next morning.

'Hurry along, everyone. Pack your readers into your bags and come and sit on the floor. I have a notice for you to take home today,' Mrs Bottomley instructed.

Clementine wondered what the notice was about. The last one had said there was an outbreak of head lice. Her mother had inspected her hair and even washed it in some special shampoo to be sure. Clementine didn't like the thought of those creatures at all. She scratched her head.

Joshua looked at her. 'Have you got nits?'

'No.' Clementine's face turned red.

'Joshua Tribble, stop talking and hurry along,' Mrs Bottomley barked.

The children quickly found a place on the floor in front of Mrs Bottomley's special chair. No one was allowed to sit on it except her.

'I have some news but it's nothing to get too excited about,' Mrs Bottomley said sternly.

Sophie and Clementine looked at each other in bewilderment. Poppy smiled.

'I don't believe for one second that this is a good idea, but I've been overruled. Miss Critchley has arranged for us to visit the farm at Highton Hall on Friday.'

A cheer went up around the room.

'Shh. Stop that nonsense immediately or I'll leave you behind on Friday to do yard duty with Mr Pickles.' The teacher's face was red and she was huffing and blowing like a steam train.

Clementine leaned around and grinned at Poppy, who beamed back.

'Did you know?' Clemmie asked.

Poppy nodded. 'Daddy said that I couldn't tell because it wasn't definite, but now it must be.'

'I love farms,' Joshua said.

'Yes, well, I don't,' Mrs Bottomley said through gritted teeth. Before she could say any more, the bell rang for the end of the school day.

The kindergarten children cheered once more, picked up their bags, and streamed out of the classroom.

'Kindergarten! Two straight lines. Now!' Mrs Bottomley called after them but the children had scattered like Mexican jumping beans.

Miss Critchley was already standing at the school gate, where she liked to farewell the students each afternoon.

'We're going to Poppy's farm, Miss Critchley,' Clementine shouted as she raced towards her.

'It's a proper 'scursion, on a bus,' Angus called after her.

'You're going to have a wonderful time,' Miss Critchley told the children. She didn't add her next thought: *Even if Mrs Bottomley came up with every excuse under the sun not to take you.*

Mrs Bottomley appeared, muttering something under her breath.

'It's lovely to see the children so excited,' said Miss Critchley.

'Yes, I suppose you'd think it is.' Mrs Bottomley's lip curled and she marched off towards the staff room.

A WILD RIDE

Clementine stood at the gate and looked for Uncle Digby's ancient Mini Minor. She couldn't see it anywhere. Her tummy began to feel funny. It wasn't like him to be late.

'Don't worry, Clementine,' said Miss Critchley. 'I'm sure someone will be here to pick you up soon. If not, you can come and wait in my office.'

Clementine smiled back at the head teacher. Miss Critchley always knew the right thing to say.

A few minutes later, Aunt Violet's shiny red car roared down the road and skidded to a halt outside the school gates.

The old woman put down the passenger side window and leaned across. 'Don't just stand there, Clementine,' she called. 'I haven't got all day.'

'I didn't know you were coming to get me this afternoon,' said Clementine as she walked towards the car.

Miss Critchley followed. She opened the back door for Clementine and leaned inside. 'Hello Miss Appleby. Thank you for picking Clementine up, but I really must insist that you observe the speed limit outside the school.'

'Oh, I can see those signs perfectly well, Miss Critchley,' Aunt Violet replied. 'It's just that I was running late and I didn't want Clementine to worry.'

Clementine was surprised to hear this.

'We'd worry a lot more if you had an accident,' Miss Critchley insisted.

'I've never had an accident in my life and

I don't plan to start now,' the old woman retorted. 'If you'd remove yourself and allow Clementine to get settled, we'll be on our way.'

Clementine hopped into the back seat and buckled her seatbelt.

'Bossy woman,' Aunt Violet muttered. 'Who does she think she is?'

'She's the head teacher, of course,' Clementine piped up, wondering why Aunt Violet had asked.

'I don't care who she is, she needn't tell me how to drive.' Aunt Violet's face furrowed into a deep frown and she pulled out from the kerb sharply. There was a blast of a horn and a screech of brakes as Joshua Tribble's father only just managed to swerve and avoid hitting the side of the car.

Aunt Violet put down the window and yelled, 'What do you think you're doing, man? You could have killed us driving like that.'

'Excuse me, lady, but you pulled out and didn't even look,' Mr Tribble yelled back.

Joshua was sitting in the passenger seat.

He pulled on his cheeks and made a monster face at Clementine.

'Why don't you control your little brat?' Aunt Violet gave Joshua a scary stare.

The boy reeled in fright and covered his eyes.

Aunt Violet harrumphed loudly, then squeezed her car through the gap and sped off.

'Where's Mummy and Uncle Digby?' Clementine asked. She was beginning to hope that Aunt Violet wouldn't pick her up too often.

'They're talking to some builders about the roof,' Aunt Violet replied. 'And not before time.'

Clementine nodded and then remembered her news. She bounced in her seat. 'We're going on an excursion!'

'Yes, lovely,' Aunt Violet said absently.

'To Poppy's farm,' Clementine went on.

'It's not Poppy's farm, Clementine. It's the Highton-Smith-Kennington-Joneses',' her great-aunt replied.

Clementine didn't know what she meant. 'But Poppy lives there.'

'Yes, because her father and mother work there,' said Aunt Violet. 'But it's not theirs.'

'Oh,' Clementine said. It didn't matter who owned it. She was just excited that the whole class was going. 'Well, we're visiting on Friday. We're going to see horses and cows and sheep and chickens. And four of our chicks hatched in class today and I got to hold the first one and give her a name. She's called Velvet.'

'Vel–' Aunt Violet began. 'Not Violet?' She glanced in the rear-vision mirror and saw Clementine frown.

'No! That's your name. Her name is Velvet,' Clementine repeated. Sometimes Aunt Violet could be so silly. 'She's brown and fluffy and her feathers feel like my velvet dress.'

Her great-aunt simply nodded.

Aunt Violet turned the car into the driveway at Penberthy House and came to a halt outside the front door. Clementine scrambled out of her seatbelt, grabbed her schoolbag and jumped out of the car, slamming the door.

'Clementine!' Aunt Violet admonished. 'I'd

like that door to remain attached to the car, thank you very much.'

'Sorry, Aunt Violet!' Clementine called back. 'Thank you for coming to get me.' She skittered up the front steps and into the house.

Violet Appleby watched as Clementine disappeared. She wondered if the child had ever been more excited about anything in her life.

A THORNY CHAT

Clementine was counting down the days to Friday. Her mother and Uncle Digby thought the excursion was a wonderful idea, and Lady Clarissa immediately signed up to help. Two other parents had volunteered to come along and assist, and of course Mr and Mrs Bauer would be at the farm too.

On Thursday afternoon, Clementine was playing in the garden at home with Lavender. 'All of the eggs have hatched now and the chicks are so sweet. They've all got names too. You already know about Velvet, Lemonade, Henny Penny and Joshua, and now there's Blackie, Chicka, Hattie and Noodle,' she babbled to the little pig. 'Mrs Bottomley doesn't seem to like the names much, and she's giving us *so* many strange lessons about our visit to Poppy's farm. We're not to get too close to the animals; we have to wash our hands after touching any animals, which is silly because I touch you all the time.' Lavender snuffled indignantly and Clementine shook her head. 'And we mustn't pick anything to eat from the garden. But isn't that what a farm is for?'

Clementine tucked a daisy behind her ear and put one behind Lavender's ear as well. 'We're going to see cows and sheep and horses and I think there could even be some pigs too. But they won't be little teacup piggies like you. Mr Bauer has great big pigs. They have chickens and ducks as well. I can't wait. Mummy's coming and I wish we could take you, but you might get lost and that would be terrible. So you have to stay here with Uncle Digby and Aunt Violet and Pharaoh.'

Clementine was admiring the new buds on her mother's favourite rosebush when she heard a loud snipping sound behind her.

'Who are you talking to, Clementine?' Aunt Violet demanded. She'd just cut a long red rose and was in the process of removing the thorns.

'Oh, hello Aunt Violet, I was just telling Lavender all about the excursion tomorrow and explaining why she can't come.'

'And do you really think the pig understands you?' her great-aunt asked as she hacked another stem.

Clementine nodded. 'Yes, of course.'

'What a lot of drivel,' Aunt Violet snorted. 'She's a pig, for heaven's sake.'

'And pigs are really smart,' Clementine replied, wrinkling her nose.

'Here, hold these.' Aunt Violet passed Clementine the roses. The child hesitated. 'It's all right. I've taken the thorns off.'

'What are they for?' Clementine buried her nose in the centre of one of the flowers. 'They smell lovely.'

'They're for my room,' Violet replied. 'It could do with some cheering up.'

'Is it sad?' Clementine asked.

The old woman looked at Clementine. 'What are you talking about this time?'

'You said that your room could do with some cheering up so I thought it must be sad,' Clementine explained.

'I just want some roses to brighten the place up. Is that all right with you?' Aunt Violet cut three more blooms.

Clementine wondered why Aunt Violet was in a bad mood this time. 'Are you sad, Aunt Violet?'

'What?'

'Are you sad?' Clementine asked again. 'Are the flowers really to cheer you up?'

'You can think whatever you like, Clementine.' Aunt Violet snatched the roses and stalked off.

Clementine watched as Aunt Violet stomped through the garden, up the back steps and into the kitchen. She waited a little while then followed. Lavender snuffled along in the grass close behind her.

In the kitchen, Uncle Digby was cutting up some apples for a pie and Clemmie's mother was stirring something on the stovetop. She looked up as Clementine entered. 'Hello Clemmie, would you like a glass of milk and some afternoon tea?'

'Yes, please.'

'I left you something to eat,' Uncle Digby said. There was half a chocolate eclair sitting underneath the cake dome.

'Yum,' the child squealed.

'The doctor said that I have to go easy on the sweet treats,' said Uncle Digby. He patted his chest above his heart. 'So I'm sharing with you.'

Clementine nodded. She didn't want Uncle Digby to have any more scares like the one he'd had a little while ago, when they'd been hosting a wedding at the house.

'Where's Aunt Violet?' she enquired.

'Oh, I don't know. I heard her come in and she hurried away upstairs. I hope she's not coming down with another one of her headaches,' said Lady Clarissa, sighing.

Digby raised his eyebrows. 'Yes, we all know what that means.'

'She can't help it if she gets nasty headaches,' Lady Clarissa told the old man.

'Did you say she can't help it if she has a nasty head?' Digby chuckled. Clementine giggled too.

'Digby Pertwhistle, you cheeky thing,' Clarissa admonished. 'I think there has been some steady improvement in Aunt Violet's behaviour recently.'

'Yes, let's just hope it continues,' he replied.

Clementine wondered whether she should run upstairs and see if her great-aunt was all right.

Lady Clarissa placed a glass of milk and the half chocolate eclair on the table in front of her daughter. 'Oh, look! Lavender, you're such a

funny little thing,' she said, turning her head towards the fireplace.

Clemmie glanced around. She couldn't see anything unusual. Lavender was just sitting in her basket with Pharaoh beside her. As she turned back to her plate, she noticed a large bite missing from her eclair. Her mother was licking her fingers and hurrying back to the stove.

'Mummy!' the girl shouted. 'You ate my eclair.'

Her mother chortled. 'Sorry, Clemmie, I couldn't help myself. It just looked too good. Besides, you don't want to spoil your dinner, do you?'

Clementine giggled. Uncle Digby was laughing too. Now, Clementine thought, if only she could get Aunt Violet to laugh more, things would be just about perfect.

'I can't wait for tomorrow,' Clementine said as she gobbled the last bite of her afternoon tea.

'I was talking with Poppy's mother this afternoon and she's very excited too. She's planning a sausage sizzle for your lunch,' said Lady Clarissa.

The telephone rang and Clementine slid off her chair and ran to pick it up.

'Good afternoon, Penberthy House, this is Clementine. How may I help you?' she said confidently. Her mother and Uncle Digby turned around and smiled at Clemmie. She was becoming very good at answering the phone and Uncle Digby said that they might have to start paying her pocket money for being the hotel receptionist.

'I'll just get Mummy,' she said, and put her hand over the mouthpiece.

'Who is it, darling?' Lady Clarissa brushed her hands against her apron and walked towards Clementine.

Clemmie shrugged. 'They didn't say.'

Lady Clarissa frowned as she took the phone. 'Good afternoon, this is Clarissa Appleby.'

Clementine and Uncle Digby couldn't help hearing Lady Clarissa's responses.

'Oh, a recommendation from Mrs Fox?

That's wonderful. Yes, it was a beautiful wedding . . . Tomorrow? I'm afraid I can't tomorrow . . . I see. I'll have to think what I can do . . . I'll just write that number down and I'll get back to you in a little while.' And with that Clarissa hung up the phone.

'That sounded interesting.' Digby was now stirring apples on the stovetop. The sugar and cloves mixed in with the simmering fruit filled the kitchen with sweet smells.

'Yes, it seems Mrs Fox has been telling people about how wonderful Harriet's wedding was. That was a lady called Mrs Wilde. She wants to come and have a look at the house for her own daughter's wedding later in the year.'

'Another wedding?' Clementine gasped. She had so enjoyed the first one and couldn't wait for there to be another.

'Yes, but I'm afraid we might not be able to do it. Her daughter has just flown in from overseas and will be here for a couple of days. They can only come tomorrow and they can't be sure what time they'll get here.'

Clementine's face fell. 'But my excursion's tomorrow.'

'I can meet with them,' Uncle Digby said.

Lady Clarissa shook her head. 'You have your appointment with the doctor and you're not missing it.'

Digby frowned. 'Oh no, I'm afraid not.'

'What about Aunt Violet?' Clementine asked hopefully. 'Couldn't she show the people around?'

Lady Clarissa and Uncle Digby looked at one another. 'I don't think that's a good idea. Aunt Violet isn't exactly our best advertisement,' her mother said.

Clementine sighed. It was true. The last time Aunt Violet had been left in charge of the guests was on the weekend of the wedding. She'd rearranged the bedroom allocations and had an awful argument with Mrs Fox.

Digby frowned. 'Surely there's some way we can manage it. That repair quote for the roof was much more than we'd expected, Clarissa. Another wedding would just about cover it.'

Clarissa nodded. For years she'd put off the huge job of re-doing the roof, and dotted buckets around the house to catch the drips each time it rained. The builder had recently discovered a rather more sinister patch of damp in one of the upstairs bedrooms and said that if she didn't have the roof repaired soon, it could collapse completely.

Clementine was thinking. She knew that getting the roof fixed was important and Uncle Digby couldn't miss his doctor's appointment.

'Do you think Aunt Violet would like to come on the excursion?' she asked.

'Well, I don't know. Would you really be happy to take Aunt Violet with you?' her mother asked.

Clementine nodded. 'It might make her feel better.'

'What do you mean, sweetheart?'

'It might cheer her up,' Clementine replied.

Clarissa still wasn't following. She didn't know if something specific had upset Aunt Violet or she was in one of her usual grumps.

'I think it's more a question of would Aunt Violet want to go?' Uncle Digby added.

'I'll ask her.' Clementine jumped off her chair and walked over to the basket near the fireplace. She reached in to pick Pharaoh up.

'What are you doing with puss?' her mother asked.

'Aunt Violet always says that Pharaoh doesn't spend much time with her any more, so I thought I'd take him upstairs so he can have a visit.'

Digby winked at Clemmie. 'Good idea.'

Clementine cradled the bald cat in her arms and walked up the back stairs towards Aunt Violet's bedroom.

'Well, that's a turn up for the books,' said Digby.

'I just hope Aunt Violet says yes,' Lady Clarissa replied.

A QUESTION

Clementine shifted Pharaoh onto one arm and knocked gently on the door of the Blue Room.

There was no answer.

'Aunt Violet,' she called. 'May I come in?'

Violet Appleby was sitting at her dressing table, arranging the roses she'd cut earlier in a pretty crystal vase.

Clementine knocked again, a little louder. She was having trouble balancing Pharaoh and knocking at the same time, and hoped Aunt Violet would hurry up and answer.

Aunt Violet caught her finger on a rogue thorn and cursed as a tiny spot of blood oozed from her skin.

'What is it now?' the old woman called.

Clementine turned the handle and entered the room.

'Phew, I thought I was going to drop him. Pharaoh wanted to say hello.' She walked across the room and deposited the cat onto her great-aunt's lap.

'Well, it's about time you paid me a visit, my boy.' Aunt Violet nuzzled her face against Pharaoh's and he began to purr.

Clementine loved his motor. It was loud, like a sports car engine. She sometimes wished Lavender could purr, but she could grunt and squeak and that was cute too.

Clementine studied the crystal bowl of roses. 'Is that Granny's vase?'

'What if it is?' Aunt Violet asked.

'It's not allowed out of the sitting room cabinet,' Clementine explained. 'Mummy says it's too valuable.'

'Well, it looks lovely right where it is and I'll thank you not to blab to your mother or Pertwhistle. I'll put it back when I'm finished with it,' said Aunt Violet tartly.

Clementine frowned. She usually told her mother and Uncle Digby everything. She didn't like the idea of keeping a secret from them.

Aunt Violet looked at Clementine. 'Is that all?'

Clemmie shook her head. 'I was wondering . . .'

There was a short silence.

'Yes, yes, what is it?' Her great-aunt sighed impatiently. 'I haven't got all day, you know. Some of us have things to do.'

Clementine wondered exactly what it was that Aunt Violet had to do. She never seemed especially busy. Not like her mother and Uncle Digby.

'Well, you know how my class is going to Poppy's farm tomorrow and Mummy is supposed to come?' Clementine said.

Aunt Violet nodded. 'Yes. So?'

'Mummy can't come any more. Someone

wants to look at the house for a wedding and she says that it's best if she's here, and Uncle Digby said you can't be trusted to talk to people after last time.'

'What? That's outrageous!' Aunt Violet snapped. 'I'll thank Pertwhistle to keep his opinions to himself.'

'But you had a fight with Mrs Fox, remember?' Clementine reminded the old woman.

Violet Appleby rolled her eyes. 'The woman was a tyrant. Why don't you take Pertwhistle? It would be good to have him out of the house. Old codger's always sneaking up on me. He gives me the willies.'

'Uncle Digby can't come because he has to go to the doctor,' Clementine said. 'So I was wondering if you would come instead.'

'Me? Go to a farm? With all those smelly children?' She wrinkled her nose. 'No. It's out of the question. I have too many things to do. Do you think I sit around the house twiddling my thumbs all day?'

Clementine didn't realise that her aunt wasn't expecting an answer. She nodded. 'You do sit around the house. I don't know about twiddling your thumbs.'

The old woman pursed her lips. 'I do not! I'll have you know that I'm a very busy person.'

'Mummy says that if you give a busy person something extra to do, they'll always fit it in,' Clementine said.

'She would say that.' Violet Appleby paused for a moment. 'Why would you want me to come anyway?'

'Because I thought it might cheer you up and it will be fun,' Clementine replied.

'Fun?' her great-aunt repeated absently. She couldn't remember the last time she'd had fun. 'No, Clementine, I can't.'

Clementine's face fell. Aunt Violet was just about the most confusing person she'd ever met. They'd had some lovely times reading books together lately and Aunt Violet had even put Clementine to bed the other week, but now she was being so mean.

'Well, I don't want you to come anyway,' Clementine whispered.

'What did you say, Clementine?'

'I don't want you to come,' the child said, a little louder.

'So you ask me and then you don't really want me at all,' her great-aunt accused. 'Well, that's lovely, that is.'

'But you said that you didn't want to and you're too busy,' Clementine said.

'Well, now I think I might.' Aunt Violet stood up and deposited Pharaoh onto the four-poster bed.

'You might what?' Clementine asked cautiously.

'I might come along, if that's all right with you, Miss Change-Your-Mind,' said Aunt Violet.

'Really? You're not just saying that?' Clementine thought it was Aunt Violet who should be called Miss Change-Your-Mind.

Aunt Violet nodded. 'I said I would. But I'd better not have to look after any of those snotty brats.'

Clementine shook her head. 'Mrs Bottomley said that she only invited parents to come because she had to. She said they really wouldn't be much use.'

Violet Appleby raised her eyebrows. 'Did she now? We'll see about that.'

Clementine didn't know if she should feel happy that Aunt Violet had said yes, or worried that it could turn out like the pet day at school. On that day, Aunt Violet and Pharaoh had won the prize for pet most like its owner, even though Aunt Violet hadn't entered the competition. But at least now her mother would be able to meet the lady about the wedding and they could get the roof fixed.

Clementine walked to the door and then turned back to Aunt Violet. The woman was flicking through a magazine. 'Are you really sure?'

'Yes,' her great-aunt replied. 'But if you don't run along, I might just change my mind.'

Clementine nodded and scurried out of the room and down the main stairs.

She stopped on the landing and looked up at the portraits hanging on the wall. 'Hello

Granny and Grandpa. Aunt Violet is coming on the farm excursion. Can you believe it?'

Clementine could have sworn that her grandfather shook his head ever so slightly.

'I hope she's on her best behaviour,' Clementine said.

Uncle Digby was standing in the hallway below. He wondered how on earth Clementine had convinced her great-aunt to say yes.

Clementine addressed her granny's portrait. 'And I hope she doesn't upset any of the animals, or Mrs Bottomley.'

Digby grinned. Aunt Violet with twenty children and Mrs Bottomley at a farm – he rather hoped that the doctor might postpone his appointment after all, because he would have liked to see that for himself.

ROLL CALL

Clementine glanced up from where she was eating her cereal at the kitchen table. 'You look nice, Aunt Violet.' Her great-aunt was wearing a white pants-suit with a pair of shiny red ballet flats. She wore a large pearl choker around her neck. 'But don't you think you might get dirty?'

'I wasn't planning on it.' The old woman pulled out a chair and sat down.

'I think Clementine's right, Aunt Violet. White on a school excursion might be a little risky,' Lady Clarissa said diplomatically. 'Especially to a farm.'

'I wear white all the time, Clarissa. I'll be fine.' Aunt Violet poured herself a cup of tea from the pot in the middle of the table.

'Until you have to feed something,' said Digby Pertwhistle. He was buttering several slices of toast.

'I won't be doing any of that,' Aunt Violet replied. 'I'm only going because Clarissa has pressing business and you have that silly doctor's appointment, which is a waste of time if you ask me. There doesn't seem to be anything wrong with you.'

'Thank you for your learned opinion, Dr Appleby,' Digby replied.

Clementine frowned. 'Are you a doctor, Aunt Violet?' This was the first she'd heard of such a thing. Her great-aunt certainly hadn't acted like a doctor when Uncle Digby had needed to go to hospital.

'No, Clementine, Uncle Digby is just teasing,' said her mother. She sat down and picked up the teapot. 'Of course he needs to go for his check-up. We wouldn't want anything to happen to him.'

'Well, that's a matter of opinion,' Aunt Violet murmured. 'Anyway, Clementine, you're not exactly in farm attire yourself.'

The children had been allowed to wear casual clothes for the day. 'This is an old dress,' Clementine replied. 'I love it but I won't be able to wear it much longer because I'm getting too big. I'm nearly five and a half now.'

'Well, it is . . . rather sweet,' her great-aunt replied.

Clementine was surprised to hear her say so.

Lady Clarissa glanced at the clock in the kitchen. 'Heavens, look at the time. Clemmie, run along and brush your teeth.'

Clementine pushed her chair out and hopped down. 'Look, our shoes match,' she said to Aunt Violet before scurrying away up the back stairs.

It wasn't long before Clementine farewelled

her mother and Uncle Digby and she and Aunt Violet were in the car heading towards Highton Mill. Clementine was glad that her great-aunt didn't seem to be in quite as much of a hurry as she was earlier in the week.

As they arrived in the street, there was an old red bus sitting outside the school gates.

'Where am I supposed to park?' Aunt Violet complained.

Clementine craned her neck to see if there were any spaces on the other side of the road. She pointed and said, 'I think there's a spot down there.'

Aunt Violet pressed her foot hard on the accelerator. There was another car heading towards them and she was determined to get to the parking space first.

'Ahh!' Clementine exclaimed and covered her eyes as Aunt Violet did a U-turn in front of the oncoming car. The old woman screeched to a halt in the space and smiled smugly.

Joshua Tribble's father rolled down the

passenger window and started shouting and gesturing wildly.

'That was my spot!' he yelled, then realised who he was speaking to. 'You again!'

Aunt Violet turned her head and looked the other way, pretending not to notice. 'I didn't see your name on it,' she said under her breath.

'I think Mr Tribble's upset,' Clementine said.

'He'll get over it.' Aunt Violet opened the driver's door and got out. Mr Tribble sped away.

Clementine hopped out onto the footpath. She slung her small pink backpack onto her shoulders and closed the door carefully.

Clementine bounced along beside her great-aunt until they reached the crossing in front of the school gates. She stopped and held out her hand.

Aunt Violet strode onto the road ahead of her.

'Aunt Violet,' Clementine called.

The old woman turned her head. 'What are you doing back there?'

'You have to hold my hand,' Clementine said. 'It's the rules.'

'Oh.' Aunt Violet walked back to the kerb. Clementine slipped her hand into Aunt Violet's.

Just inside the school gates, a crowd of children and a small group of parents milled about. Mrs Bottomley was there too, armed with a large clipboard and with a floppy straw hat on her head.

Aunt Violet narrowed her eyes. 'Good heavens, what is that woman wearing?'

It seemed that Mrs Bottomley had abandoned her usual brown checked suit in favour of a pair of brown corduroy trousers and a pasty-looking beige shirt. On her feet she wore dark green wellington boots. She'd been up before dawn going over the plans for the day and couldn't understand why her tummy was a little knotted. The thought occurred to her that she had always felt that way as a child, just before something exciting was about to happen. But surely that couldn't be the reason for her discomfort.

'Good morning, everyone,' the teacher called over the din. 'I need you to make two straight lines, in alphabetical order.'

Several of the children began to move. The parents, most of whom had come to wave the group off, continued chatting. Clementine looked up at Aunt Violet and pulled her towards the teacher.

Ethel Bottomley surveyed the chaotic scene in front of her and raised the whistle around her neck to her lips. The shrill squeal silenced everyone and she repeated her instruction.

'Children, two straight lines. NOW!' The whole class scampered into formation. They were so used to lining up in alphabetical order by now that it took no longer than half a minute. The parents didn't know what to do, so they stood at the back.

'We need to mark the roll,' Mrs Bottomley said. 'Clementine Appleby.'

'Yes, Mrs Bottomley,' Clemmie said.

'Angus Archibald,' Mrs Bottomley continued.

'Yes, Na–'

His grandmother shot him a nasty look.

'I mean, Mrs Bottomley,' Angus replied.

The teacher called each name until the whole class was checked off.

'I don't know why she couldn't have just counted you all,' Aunt Violet whispered to Clementine.

Clementine looked up. 'But she always calls the roll.'

'It wastes an awful lot of time, if you ask me,' Aunt Violet said.

Clementine could only agree. She'd thought that from her first day.

'Now the parents,' Mrs Bottomley began. 'If you're not joining us, please move away from the children.'

'Godfathers,' Aunt Violet muttered. 'Is the woman incapable of counting a handful of adults?'

'Lady Appleby?'

'It's Miss Appleby and yes,' Aunt Violet replied tersely.

Ethel Bottomley looked up from where she was ticking off the list of names.

'No, you're not coming. Clementine's mother is joining us.'

'There's been a change of plans,' Aunt Violet replied. 'My niece has been caught up at home and I will be coming instead.'

Mrs Bottomley's lips twitched. 'But I was expecting Lady Appleby.'

'Well, you'll just have to make do with Miss Appleby instead,' said Aunt Violet.

'You're not exactly dressed for it,' Mrs Bottomley scolded.

Aunt Violet looked the teacher up and down and sneered. 'I don't know, Mrs Bottomley. Someone needed to inject a little bit of style into this occasion. Clearly that wasn't on your agenda.'

Ethel Bottomley frowned. She decided to ignore the woman's last comment.

Sophie's mother, Odette, was there too, along with Joshua Tribble's father. Mrs Bauer and her husband would meet the group at the farm with Poppy, who'd been allowed to stay home that morning.

'All right, everyone, before we get on the bus I want to go over our list of rules,' Mrs

Bottomley barked. 'Who can tell me one of them?'

Hands shot into the air.

'Yes, Sophie?' The woman pointed at the dark-haired child.

'Don't wander off.'

'Good. Anyone else?'

'Don't touch the animals,' another voice called.

Mrs Bottomley nodded.

'Don't eat anything from the garden,' Astrid said.

'Yes, I don't want anyone getting sick,' Mrs Bottomley replied.

Violet Appleby raised her hand.

The teacher wondered what the old woman had to offer. She hesitated then pointed at her.

'Don't have any fun,' Aunt Violet said with a straight face. There was a titter of laughter from the other parents and some of the children.

'Of course we're going to have fun, Miss Appleby. Orderly fun,' Mrs Bottomley sneered.

'It doesn't sound like much fun to me,' Aunt Violet scoffed. 'Fancy going to a farm and telling the children they can't touch the animals. The only reason I agreed to Clementine's request to come along was that she told me there was fun in the offing. I'm not hearing that at the moment.'

Joshua's father leaned over to Sophie's mother and whispered, 'I never imagined Miss Appleby and I would agree on anything, but the woman's quite right.'

Odette Rousseau chuckled.

Clementine wished that Aunt Violet would stop talking. She could see Mrs Bottomley's ears turning pink and she looked crosser than usual.

'First and foremost, Miss Appleby, it is my duty to ensure that the children in my care are safe at all times. And that they learn something. Now if you're quite finished, you can board the bus.'

THE BUS RIDE

Clementine walked up the steps. A round man wearing a brown shirt and shorts, and long beige socks was sitting behind the steering wheel. He had curly brown hair too, and Clementine wondered if he was related to Mrs Bottomley.

'Good morning, miss,' the man said with a smile. 'My name's Bernie Stubbs.'

'Good morning,' Clementine smiled back.

'I think we're in for a good day,' he said and gave her a wink.

Clementine decided then that he couldn't be related to Mrs Bottomley. He was much too happy and friendly.

She walked into the aisle and wondered where to sit. Aunt Violet, who had entered the bus behind her, had already made up her mind.

'Clementine, here,' her great-aunt said as she slid into the front seat on the passenger side.

'But Mrs Bottomley said that we have to keep the front seats free for people who get bus sick,' Clementine protested.

'I don't care what Mrs Bottomley said. We're sitting here.' Aunt Violet pursed her lips and Clementine slipped in beside her. 'I'm not going any further into this contraption than is absolutely necessary.'

The other children streamed onto the vehicle and raced towards the back. By the time Mrs Bottomley walked up the steps everyone had found a seat – although Joshua and Angus were playing a rowdy game and rushing up and down the aisle.

'You boys stop that at once,' Mrs Bottomley shouted, then blew her whistle. Joshua and Angus sat behind Mr Tribble, who had been trying unsuccessfully to get the two boys to settle down.

Mrs Bottomley gave him a stern look and then glanced at Aunt Violet. She was about to say something but Aunt Violet got in first.

'Clementine mentioned that the front seats were reserved for people who weren't good travellers,' the old woman said. 'And we wouldn't want anyone in the back of the bus to suffer if someone's feeling a bit peaky.' Aunt Violet motioned at Clementine, and Mrs Bottomley kept her mouth closed. She could have sworn that there was nothing on the child's medical form about travel sickness but she didn't feel like having another argument with Miss Appleby.

The driver, who had hopped off the bus to make some last-minute checks, reappeared and lumbered back to his seat.

'Good morning, Ethel. You're looking lovely today,' he said, grinning at Mrs Bottomley.

A crimson flush rose on Mrs Bottomley's cheeks and she giggled like a schoolgirl. No one had told her that in years.

The bus driver turned the key in the ignition and the vehicle sputtered.

'All aboard?' he asked, glancing at Mrs Bottomley.

'Wait a minute. I have to call the roll.'

'Again?' Aunt Violet said. 'Surely you could just count everyone.'

Ethel Bottomley held onto her clipboard like a drowning sailor to a lifebuoy. She pulled out her pen.

'Would you like this?' Mr Stubbs offered her a small microphone.

Mrs Bottomley took it from him and pushed the button on the side of the handpiece. It crackled to life.

'When everyone is in their seats I will do a final check of the roll before we head off.'

There was an audible groan from Aunt Violet, and Mrs Bottomley noticed that Mr Tribble rolled his eyes too.

She ignored them both and ran down the list, checking off the names.

'All present and accounted for,' said Mrs Bottomley, tapping her pen on the page.

The bus lurched forward and Mrs Bottomley wobbled on her feet.

'Heavens, Mr Stubbs, you could have waited a moment.' Mrs Bottomley clutched the pole beside the driver and swung into her seat behind him. 'I almost ended up in your lap.'

'That wouldn't have been so bad now, Ethel, would it?' he chuckled.

'I think you should keep your eyes on the road, driver,' Aunt Violet said loudly.

Ethel Bottomley's face was redder than a beetroot. She ignored Miss Appleby's comment and set to arranging her handbag beside her.

Clementine looked out of the window as the bus passed by the little row of shops where Sophie's father had his patisserie. Her tummy fluttered. She turned to her great-aunt and declared, 'Today is going to be fun!'

Her great-aunt nodded. 'If you say so.'

Clementine reached out and put her hand into Aunt Violet's. To her surprise, the old woman gave it a squeeze.

The bus bumped along to the other side of the village. The farm at Highton Hall wasn't too far away but required the driver to navigate some narrow country lanes.

'Perhaps we should have a song,' Sophie's mother suggested loudly. She started a rousing chorus of 'The Wheels on the Bus'.

Mrs Bottomley leaned forward and gestured at the microphone. 'Give me that, Mr Stubbs.'

He grinned in the rear-vision mirror. 'Oh good, are we going to have some karaoke?'

'Certainly not,' said the teacher. 'Children, please stop that singing at once. You're distracting Mr Stubbs.'

'Oh no, I love a good singalong,' the driver protested.

'You're not being very helpful, Mr Stubbs,' Mrs Bottomley whispered.

'I just thought it would be nice to have a song,' the man replied.

'Goodness no,' Ethel Bottomley said quietly, then looked over at Clementine. 'Children, all this noise is, um, upsetting Clementine. We don't want to make her sick, do we?'

'But I don't get bus–' Clementine began to protest then felt a nudge from her great-aunt.

Aunt Violet gave Clemmie a freezing stare. The singing stopped. For a few minutes all that could be heard was the drone of the engine as Mr Stubbs wrestled the old beast down a gear and headed up the hill.

Soon the bus slowed and Mr Stubbs turned off the road and through a grand set of gates. They were now on the estate of Highton Hall.

The main house was quite a distance away, through another set of gates on the left. But the bus continued right, down a tree-lined drive dappled with sunlight. They passed several cottages and at the end of the road, the bus pulled up outside a hotchpotch of sheds.

'Look, there's Poppy!' Clementine exclaimed as her friend came running towards them.

The atmosphere on the bus had risen to fever pitch with everyone jostling to see what was going on outside.

'There's a duck,' one of the boys called.

'I can see a cow over there,' another child shouted.

'Children, get back into your seats and sit down,' Mrs Bottomley yelled. She snatched the microphone before Mr Stubbs had time to pass it to her.

She instructed the children to stay where they were and then hopped off the bus to find Mr Bauer, who would be taking the group on a tour of the farm. She was eager to go over the schedule with him one last time. Poppy said hello and Heinrich Bauer appeared from around the side of one of the sheds.

'Good morning, Mrs Bottomley,' he said in his thick German accent. 'It is good to see you.'

'Yes,' said Mrs Bottomley. 'I suppose I should thank you for inviting us.'

'I see the children are excited.' Mr Bauer

nodded towards the bus, which had lots of little faces pressed up against the windows.

'A little too excited for my liking,' Mrs Bottomley replied. 'You'll need to take a firm hand with them, Mr Bauer. I certainly will. If anyone gets up to mischief they'll be locked up in the dairy.'

'Don't worry, Mrs Bottomley. The children will be fine. I have lots of things for them to see and they will be too tired to get up to any mischief-making.'

Mrs Bottomley reached for her schedule but the man had already jumped onto the bus and begun to welcome the children loudly.

'My name is Heinrich Bauer and you know my little girl, Poppy,' he said. 'Now we are going to have a lovely time on the farm today but you must make sure that you follow my instructions. Most of all, I want everyone to have some fun today.'

Aunt Violet was glad to hear it. At least Mr Bauer seemed excited to have the children visiting.

GRANNY BERT

A little way back down the lane was Rose Cottage. It was home to Albertine Rumble, known to almost everyone in the district as Granny Bert. As the old red bus clunked by, the woman woke from a nap and remembered that Lily Bauer had invited her to morning tea. Her granddaughter Daisy had already left for work at the doctor's surgery. The girl assisted Dr Everingham in Highton Mill three days a week and helped out at Highton Hall two other days.

Daisy had helped choose her grandmother's clothes that morning and left her with some sandwiches for her lunch. She hated leaving the old woman on her own, as Granny seemed to be getting more and more forgetful by the day. But at least Lily and Heinrich were close by and Mrs Greening, who lived with her husband in the Gatehouse, often dropped in to check on her too.

Granny Bert pulled on her cardigan and gathered up her handbag and walking stick. She never went anywhere without either one. She wobbled her way downstairs and out through the back door, taking the path to the front of the cottage. She was surprised to see a bus parked beside the hay shed and wondered where it had come from. Granny walked towards it and saw that the door was open. She poked her head inside and drew in a deep breath. There was something about the smell that brought back all sorts of memories.

She used to ride on the bus all the time. She'd go into the village, and sometimes much further, to see her sister who lived in Downsfordvale. Granny Bert smiled to herself, remembering the lovely feeling of the bus swaying and the excitement of a new adventure.

Lily Bauer had been rushing about all morning. She was just about to take the brownies out of the oven when Poppy called out that the bus had arrived. At least she had a few minutes to spare while Heinrich organised the children. He said that he'd take them straight to the henhouse to collect the eggs, which she planned to boil up and have as part of their lunch.

Her brownies looked perfect and smelt delicious. She popped them on the sink to cool and checked on the scones she'd baked earlier, scurrying about to fill the jam and cream pots.

Having awoken to a sky as big and blue as the sea, she'd asked Heinrich to set up a row of trestle tables outside, which she planned to use at morning tea and lunch. They'd had the hay shed on standby in case of bad weather but it looked as if they'd be able to enjoy the outdoors. There were enough chairs for the adults but the children would have to sit on the grass. Lily didn't think they'd mind.

She wondered if she'd have time to pop over and get Granny Bert. The woman had never fully recovered from a bout of illness earlier in the year and she certainly wasn't the same robust old lady they knew and loved.

Lily glanced at the clock and decided that Granny would have to make her own way over from Rose Cottage if she remembered, or no one would be getting fed at all.

SCRAMBLED EGGS

Heinrich Bauer led his visitors through the gate and around the back of the pretty stone cottage the Bauers called home. Clementine stood beside Sophie and Poppy. The three girls giggled with excitement.

Suddenly, Poppy whispered, 'What's your Aunt Violet doing here?' She had just noticed the old woman chatting to the other parents.

'I asked her,' said Clementine.

Poppy frowned. 'Why?'

'Mummy had an important meeting and Uncle Digby had to go to the doctor and I thought she might like to come.'

'Is she going to be nice?' Poppy asked.

'I hope so. But you can never tell with Aunt Violet. She's unper . . . un-pre-dictable. But she was good on the bus.'

Mr Bauer told the children about some of the plans for the morning. 'We will be having a look at the chickens and the pigs and I think we might even find someone to help milk the cow.'

'Cool!' Joshua said. 'That'll be me.'

Mrs Bottomley was standing right behind the boy. 'We'll see about that,' she replied.

'If you will follow me, we will see if the chickens have been busy this morning,' said Heinrich.

'Two straight lines,' Mrs Bottomley called as she watched the children amble off. She blew loudly on her whistle. 'Where are your partners?'

'The woman will give herself an aneurysm,' Aunt Violet whispered. Joshua Tribble's father was standing right beside her, and chortled to himself.

Aunt Violet turned and stared.

'I didn't think I'd like you at all, you old parking-spot thief! But you're actually quite funny,' he said.

Aunt Violet rolled her eyes. 'You haven't heard the half of it.'

Lily Bauer came out of the kitchen and said hello. She advised Mrs Bottomley that there were tea and scones for the adults in the garden.

The teacher shook her head sharply. 'We must go with the children.'

'You told the children the parents wouldn't be any use on the excursion anyway,' said Aunt Violet archly. 'So I'm happy to accept your invitation, Mrs Bauer. A cup of tea is just what's needed.'

'I did no such thing,' insisted Mrs Bottomley. She was trying to remember if she'd actually said that out loud at any point. She knew she'd thought it.

At the far end of the garden, Mr Bauer was leading the children towards a high stone wall. The henhouse was on the other side. He opened a timber door set into the stone and called, 'Come on, everyone.' Mrs Bottomley was trotting behind them, doing her best to catch up.

'Wow, it's like a hotel for hens,' one of the little boys exclaimed.

'Thank you, young man,' Heinrich said, grinning. 'We are very proud of our chickens. They give us eggs for the whole estate.'

Mrs Bottomley was horrified to see that Mr Bauer had taken all of the children inside the henhouse. She stood back from the doorway and crowed, 'Mr Bauer, do you think it's a good idea to have those children in there with all of those feathers and claws?'

'Of course, Mrs Bottomley,' the man called back. 'Please come inside and shut the door.'

Rows of hens – white, black, grey and red – sat in their boxes, clucking away.

Heinrich pointed at a pretty black speckled

hen, which was making a very loud noise. 'Can anyone tell me what she is doing in there?'

'She's tired,' Angus said.

Heinrich shook his head. 'No, I don't think so.'

'She's lazy,' Joshua called.

'B-cark, b-cark, b-cark.' The hen's clucking was getting louder and higher with each call.

Clementine put up her hand and waited to be asked.

Heinrich pointed to her. 'Yes, Clementine.'

'I think she's just laid an egg,' Clementine replied.

Heinrich walked up to the box and reached in underneath the fowl. He pulled out a light-brown egg.

Everyone cheered.

'Would you like to hold it, Clementine?' Mr Bauer asked. She nodded and held out her hands. Heinrich placed the egg down gently.

'It's warm,' Clementine said with a grin.

'I need some helpers to collect the eggs today,' the man said. He picked up three wicker baskets.

Everyone wanted to have a turn, so Heinrich asked Mrs Bottomley to choose six children who could go to different parts of the henhouse.

'Astrid. You can choose someone to take with you,' Mrs Bottomley said. Astrid selected Sophie.

Next, the teacher called to the tallest lad in the class, who seemed to wear a permanent frown. 'Lester, you can choose someone as well.' The boy pointed at Eddie Whipple.

'And Angus, why don't you ask someone to help you too,' Mrs Bottomley finished.

Joshua was ready to jump as soon as Angus said his name. But this time, Angus didn't.

'Angus, who would you like to be your helper?' Mrs Bottomley asked again.

The curly-haired boy pointed.

'Clementine,' Angus said.

Joshua snorted loudly.

Clementine was surprised to hear her name. She wondered if he'd meant to say it.

Joshua kicked at the dirt. 'That's his girl-friend.'

'Is not.' Angus shot Joshua a sneer.

No one else said a word.

Heinrich handed out the baskets and nodded at Mrs Bottomley. While the teacher watched the six children make their way through the henhouse, he took the rest of the class out through another door to show them where the geese slept each evening. Apparently they were roaming around the bottom field, nowhere near the henhouse. This was just as well, as Mrs Bottomley felt very uneasy about the geese. The creatures had a bad reputation for behaving like guard dogs, and she wasn't keen for her students to disturb them.

Inside with the chickens, Angus had found three eggs already and Clementine spotted another two. Clementine made sure that she deposited each new egg slowly, so it didn't clunk against the others. Angus did the same. They continued checking each box.

At the other end of the building, Astrid and Sophie were excitedly counting their eggs

and Eddie and Lester were going about their business very seriously too.

Heinrich reappeared and beckoned the children to come out and show the rest of the class their treasures.

Astrid and Sophie had eight eggs, Eddie and Lester had collected nine and Angus and Clementine had found a record-breaking thirteen.

The class was very impressed with the haul.

'I know that seems like a lot,' Heinrich explained. 'But many people live on the estate. Lily makes up cartons and delivers them to Mrs Oliver up at the Hall, Mrs Greening and Granny Bert, and if there are too many we give them to the neighbours as well. We seem to get through them and it's bad news if the girls stop laying. Last year they went on strike for a month and there were no eggs for anyone.'

'Why did they do that?' Astrid asked. 'Did they want a better henhouse?'

Heinrich Bauer smiled. 'No, they already

have the best henhouse. I discovered Mr Fox was paying them a visit each night. He couldn't get in but he spent a long time staring at the girls. I think it made them very nervous.'

'Did you shoot him?' Joshua asked. 'Because I would shoot him.'

Sophie frowned at him. 'What with? Your water pistol?'

Heinrich Bauer shook his head. 'Mr Fox has been relocated.'

Clementine wondered what that meant.

'Children, would you carry the eggs up to the house and leave them at the back door for Lily?' Heinrich directed.

Mrs Bottomley could sniff an impending disaster. 'Do you really think that's a good idea, Mr Bauer?'

'It will be fine,' the man replied.

The egg collectors walked in pairs on either side of their baskets, carrying their treasures carefully. Clementine and Angus were the last to go, and just as Clementine was walking past Joshua, the boy stretched out his foot.

'Ahhhh!' Clementine cried out as she thudded to the ground. The eggs spilled everywhere, splattering all over the lawn and on Angus's t-shirt as well.

'Why did you do that?' Angus yelled at Clementine and scrambled to his feet.

'I didn't.' Clemmie began to cry.

'What in heaven's name?' Mrs Bottomley swooped on the pair. 'What a mess! What a disaster! I knew the children couldn't be trusted with the eggs.'

Angus turned on Clementine. 'It was her fault. She tripped over and then she made me fall over too.'

Joshua had rushed ahead as soon as the pair had fallen and was now watching the drama and chuckling behind his hands.

'It was Joshua,' Clementine wailed. 'He tripped me.'

'Never mind,' Heinrich said. 'It was an accident.' He looked at Clementine's big blue eyes.

'I . . . I . . . I'm sorry,' she sobbed. 'I didn't mean to.'

'Of course you didn't mean to.' Heinrich patted the girl on the shoulder.

'I saw him,' Sophie told Clementine. 'Joshua tripped you over on purpose.'

'I did not,' Joshua lied. 'I wasn't even near her.'

Poppy stared at the boy, whose tongue shot out at her like the sneaky snake that he was.

'Angus doesn't believe me,' Clementine said.

'Don't worry about him,' said Sophie.

The children walked up to the back of the house where Lily had organised some fruit and brownies for their morning tea.

Lily took one look at Clementine and ex-claimed, 'Oh dear, what's happened, Clemmie?' The little girl began to cry again.

'I smashed the eggs,' Clemmie sobbed.

'But it was an accident, I'm sure,' Lily said as she hugged Clementine.

'Look what she did to me,' Angus exclaimed. Raw egg dripped from his t-shirt.

'Never mind.' Odette Rousseau came to the

boy's rescue. 'I'm sure we can get that off. I'll get some wipes.'

Joshua Tribble was enjoying the scene in front of him. If Angus was going to choose a girl instead of him, then he'd have to pay for his decisions. His father noticed his smug smile and stalked across the yard, eager to find out if his son had been involved. Fortunately, the man wasn't easily fooled.

Aunt Violet approached Lily and Clementine.

'I remember breaking eggs once when I was your age. And I can tell you that your great-grandmother was much more concerned about it than Mr and Mrs Bauer. It might have had something to do with the timing, as Mama was hosting a dinner party for the Highton-Smiths that very evening and wanted her cook to show off all manner of tasty treats. I was sent to bed without any dinner.'

Clementine looked at her great-aunt and sniffled. 'Really?'

'I certainly was,' the old woman said. She

pulled a handkerchief from her pocket and dabbed at Clemmie's face.

'That sounds an entirely suitable punishment for today's behaviour,' Mrs Bottomley chimed in. 'Clementine, I think you can forget about having any of those brownies Mrs Bauer has made. You need to be more careful and less wasteful.'

'How dare you.' Aunt Violet drew herself up and stood over the stout teacher. 'It was an accident. Clementine is clearly sorry about what happened and she will eat exactly what the other children are eating.'

Mrs Bottomley was about to argue when she saw Joshua Tribble laughing loudly and pointing at Clementine.

'We'll discuss it later,' the old woman huffed, and bustled away.

'No, we won't!' Aunt Violet barked after her.

PIGS AND COWS

Clementine nibbled her chocolate brownie, wondering if Mrs Bottomley was going to appear at any moment and take it from her. Aunt Violet was keeping an eye on the situation too, determined that the woman would do no such thing.

Fortunately, the teacher was caught up sorting out a disagreement between some other children.

After morning tea, Mrs Bottomley insisted that everyone go to the toilet, including the parents. There would be no accidents on her watch. Unfortunately, the queue was rather long and the group was running far behind Mrs Bottomley's schedule.

'Two straight lines, children. Now!' the woman snapped before blowing her whistle.

'Godfathers!' Aunt Violet muttered. 'Does she really need to do that?'

Clementine rushed to her place at the head of the line, beside Angus. Despite Mrs Rousseau's best efforts with a wet wipe, his shirt was still splattered with egg yolk and starting to smell nasty too.

'I'm sorry about before,' Clementine whispered.

Angus shrugged. He didn't want to talk about it.

'Will the parents be joining us this time?' Mrs Bottomley called. It wasn't really a question.

Aunt Violet had been quite happy sitting in the sun, but as the other adults moved off she thought she'd better go too.

Lily Bauer looked around and realised that

Granny Bert had never arrived. 'Heinrich, I'm just going to see Granny Bert.'

'Oh, good idea, we forgot about her,' the man replied.

'I suspect she might have forgotten about us too,' Lily said hopefully.

'What are we doing now?' Sophie asked Heinrich.

'We will go to see the pigs,' he replied.

Sophie smiled.

The class followed Heinrich Bauer in two straight lines to the pigpen that was attached to the end of the barn. His wife walked with them then shot off down the lane to Rose Cottage to find Granny Bert.

The pigpen had a shelter in the corner, and water and feed troughs near the fence. A huge mother pig lay on some scattered straw with six piglets attached to her teats and suckling noisily. Over by the fence was a large mud puddle. Judging by the crusty patchwork of brown on the sow's body, she had enjoyed rolling in it.

Joshua held his nose. 'Pooh! They stink!'

'Does anyone know what pigs eat?' Heinrich asked, ignoring the lad's antics.

'Girls,' Joshua said.

Mrs Bottomley glared at the boy. Joshua's father poked him in the back and shook his head.

Heinrich pointed at Astrid, whose hand had been the first to go up.

'Pigs are omnivorous, which means they can eat vegetables and meat. Mostly people feed them vegetable scraps from the kitchen,' Astrid said. 'But the piglets are drinking milk from their mother.'

Heinrich nodded. 'You're a clever girl. We also give our pigs some kibble that we feed the dogs.'

'And sometimes they eat cupcakes,' Clementine announced.

'How ridiculous, Clementine.' Mrs Bottomley rolled her eyes. 'Pigs do not eat cupcakes.'

'Lavender does. She loves them, but we only let her have one on special occasions, like when it's someone's birthday.'

'Your pig is hardly the same as a farm pig, is she?' Mrs Bottomley said.

'Our pigs have been known to get the odd cake every now and then,' Heinrich confirmed. He grinned and continued, 'Mostly when Mrs Greening has been experimenting with her baking and things haven't turned out so well.'

Clementine smiled at Mr Bauer, who winked at her. Mrs Bottomley didn't know anything about pigs, Clemmie thought with satisfaction.

'Why are they so dirty?' one of the children called out.

'Pigs like to bathe in the mud because they don't sweat the way people do. It's a way for them to cool down. And it looks like fun too, don't you think?' Heinrich explained.

Some of the children nodded.

'Who'd like to hold one of the piglets?' Heinrich asked.

'I don't think that's a good idea, Mr Bauer,' Mrs Bottomley replied.

'It's all right, Mrs Bottomley. Good old Marta

would probably appreciate a rest for a few minutes.'

'No,' Mrs Bottomley protested. 'The children will get dirty.'

'But I love mud,' Joshua called.

A chorus of 'Me too!' went up.

Before she could say another word, Mr Bauer entered the pigpen and snatched up one of the wriggling piglets. It squeaked and oinked and the children laughed at all the noises it made.

The mother pig, Marta, raised her head, stared briefly at Mr Bauer, then laid it down again. The poor sow looked exhausted.

'Come along, Mrs Bottomley, would you like to hold her first?'

'No, no, get her away from me.' Ethel Bottomley waved her hands and ran in a circle with Mr Bauer and the piglet chasing after her.

'Come now, the teacher must set the good example for the students. She won't hurt you.'

The children roared with laughter. Mrs Bottomley turned around and Heinrich thrust the piglet into her arms.

'What do I do with her?' The woman grimaced and held tight to the squealing beast.

'Give her a cuddle, Mrs Bottomley,' Heinrich laughed.

'I'm not cuddling a pig,' the woman squawked.

'Oh, for goodness sake, give it to me.' Aunt Violet strode forward and snatched the creature from the teacher's hands.

Clementine's mouth gaped open.

Aunt Violet then passed the piglet to Clementine, who cradled the small pink beast in her arms.

'Settle down, little piggy,' Clemmie cooed. She tickled the creature under the chin. Much to everyone's surprise, it stopped wriggling and looked up at the girl.

'You have the magic touch, Clementine,' announced Heinrich. 'She knows you like pigs.'

Mrs Bottomley shot Aunt Violet a dirty look.

The children took turns holding the piglets.

'Thank you, Aunt Violet,' Clementine whispered to the old woman. Aunt Violet was

standing at the back of the group and watching the children as they delighted in holding the wriggling creatures.

'Think nothing of it, Clementine,' Aunt Violet replied. 'Your teacher was being ridiculous.'

Mrs Bottomley glared at Aunt Violet then glanced at her watch. 'Mr Bauer, we need to be getting a move on, don't you think?'

Heinrich nodded. 'Okay, children, piggies back to their mother. We are going to meet Constance now.'

'Who's Constance?' Joshua asked.

'Constance the cow,' Poppy replied.

Mrs Bottomley led the way into the yard. She blew on her whistle and the children hurried into formation.

'Surely the children can walk from one shed to another without the military parade,' Aunt Violet muttered. She didn't realise that Mrs Bottomley, like most teachers, had powerful hearing.

'I'd prefer we didn't lose anyone, Miss

Appleby,' Mrs Bottomley replied. 'If that's all right with you.'

Aunt Violet sighed and rolled her eyes.

The group marched towards the cowshed, where they found Constance. She was a beautiful tan-coloured jersey cow, and Clementine thought she had the longest eyelashes she'd ever seen.

'She's so pretty,' Sophie said.

Clementine nodded.

'Yes, doesn't know how lucky she is with those lashes,' Aunt Violet added.

The children stood on the railings surrounding the pen while Heinrich organised himself with a tiny three-legged stool and a stainless steel bucket.

'Who would like to help me milk Constance?' he asked.

Hands shot into the air from every direction.

The man grinned at the children. 'I don't think we'll ask Mrs Bottomley this time.'

'Yes, well, I'll thank you not to,' the old woman said through pursed lips.

'What about you, Miss Appleby? Would you like to go first and show the children how it's done?'

Aunt Violet frowned. She was about to say 'no' when the word 'yes' escaped from her lips.

Clementine looked at her great-aunt in amazement. 'Are you sure?'

'Well, I don't know, Clementine, but it doesn't look too difficult.'

Aunt Violet walked through the gate into the pen. She stroked Connie's forehead and looked into the old girl's eyes.

'Hello gorgeous,' she whispered, then ran her hand along the cow's bulging body.

'I think, Miss Appleby, you have done this before?' Heinrich said.

'A long time ago, Mr Bauer.' She crouched on the stool and positioned the shiny silver bucket under Connie's udder. She placed her hand on one of the beast's teats and pulled gently. A white stream pinged against the bottom of the bucket.

The children were mesmerised as they watched. The old woman was using both hands now and the bucket was filling fast.

'Miss Appleby, you are an expert,' Heinrich told Aunt Violet, who looked up with a sheepish grin.

'Not an expert, Mr Bauer, but not bad for an old lady,' she replied.

Clementine couldn't believe it. Aunt Violet was full of surprises today.

'Who'd like to go next?' the farmer asked.

There was no shortage of volunteers. Mr Bauer picked Ella, who was happy to receive some instruction from Aunt Violet. The woman seemed very pleased to be able to help each child as they came to have their turn.

Last of all Joshua slid onto the stool.

Aunt Violet had retreated to the other end of the shed to wash her hands, so Mr Bauer tried to instruct Joshua on his milking technique. The boy pulled down hard on one of Connie's teats with no luck. He pulled again.

Mrs Bottomley was hovering close by, as the

boy had been making a particular nuisance of himself. He'd been poking and pinching the other children and his father had very little control over him. He was lucky to be getting a turn at all.

'It's not fair, she's run out of milk,' Joshua complained.

He pulled again and tilted the teat upwards. This time a long stream of milk shot out, straight at Mrs Bottomley. It hit her right in the face.

Joshua laughed loudly.

'Joshua Tribble,' the woman bellowed as she wiped the milk from her cheek. 'Stop that at once.'

The boy was tempted to have another go. He looked around and saw his father glaring.

'Don't you even think about it, young man,' Mr Tribble growled.

Connie had stood patiently chewing on her cud for almost twenty minutes. But Mr Bauer noticed that her tail had begun to twitch.

'Mrs Bottomley, you should come away from there,' the man said.

'What is it now?'

The old woman turned just in time to see Connie lift her tail and deposit a stream of runny poo on the straw behind her.

'Arrrrgh!' Mrs Bottomley shrieked and jumped clear just as the mound began to build.

'Pooh! She stinks,' Joshua called out.

'Joshua Tribble, I do not stink,' Mrs Bottomley barked.

'I meant the cow,' he said. 'But your boots stink too.' The lad pointed at the teacher's wellington boots, which were now splattered brown as well.

Mrs Bottomley shook her head and stalked to the other end of the barn to look for a tap.

Heinrich Bauer took over and finished the last few minutes of milking, then carried the pail to the gate.

'What's next?' Clementine asked excitedly. She was having a wonderful day, despite the egg incident.

Lily Bauer came racing towards the group. 'Heinrich! I can't find Granny anywhere,' she puffed. 'I've been through Rose Cottage from top to bottom; I've scoured the sheds and called Daisy, and she said that Granny should be here.'

'Did you telephone the Hall and see if she's gone up there?' her husband asked.

'Yes, and I've spoken to Mrs Greening. No one has seen her at all,' Lily replied.

'I saw an old lady when we got here, near the bus,' said Joshua.

'What was she doing near the bus?' Heinrich asked.

'She was looking inside the door, when we were walking towards the house,' the boy replied.

'Oh dear, you don't think she could have hopped on and gone to the village with Mr Stubbs, do you?' Lily asked her husband.

'Who knows?' he said. 'But I don't have time to look for her now. I have to get the barbecue started for the sausage sizzle.'

'I'll call Mr Greening and see if he can head into town and look for her,' said Lily. 'Mrs

Greening said that she and Mrs Shillingsworth would go out on foot to look.'

'And we can help with the food,' Mr Tribble spoke up. Sophie's mother nodded too.

'Well, what am I supposed to do with the children?' Mrs Bottomley asked. She had returned to the group and was most unimpressed. Lost old ladies were not on her schedule.

'You could still go and see the lambs in the field,' Heinrich suggested.

Mrs Bottomley shook her head, aghast. 'We're not going on our own! It says here that someone called Mr Greening was going to take us to view the lambs.'

'Well, I'm afraid that we need him to go and search for Granny Bert. She's a frail old lady who hasn't been herself lately and we don't want anything to happen to her. I'm sure you can understand that,' Heinrich explained.

Ethel Bottomley just wanted a cup of tea and a lie down.

Aunt Violet intervened. 'We can find our way

to the field and back, Mrs Bottomley. It would be such a pity for the children to miss out on seeing the lambs.'

'No, we're staying here,' said Mrs Bottomley.

Aunt Violet looked at the children. 'Who wants to see the new lambs?' she asked.

'Me!' the children called in unison.

'I think you're outvoted, Mrs Bottomley.' Aunt Violet smiled at the woman and arched her eyebrow. 'Besides, Poppy lives on the farm. I'm sure we won't get lost with her in the lead.'

Poppy nodded like a jack-in-the-box. 'I know the farm backwards,' she confirmed.

'And me and Sophie have been here before,' Clementine added.

'Sophie and I, Clementine,' Mrs Bottomley corrected.

'That's settled, then. Let's go and find some lambs,' Aunt Violet commanded, as the children cheered.

LAMB TALES

The group set off with Poppy and Aunt Violet in the lead and Mrs Bottomley bringing up the rear. Joshua's father and Sophie's mother stayed behind to help with lunch and the search for Granny Bert.

The children would be having barbecued sausages in bread rolls baked fresh at Sophie's father's patisserie, salad from the garden, hard-boiled eggs from the chickens and milkshakes courtesy of Constance the cow for their lunch. Mrs Greening, who lived with her husband in the Gatehouse on the estate, had made one of her delicious cakes too. Nearly all of the food was from the farm.

Poppy led the class through a gate in the stone wall at the front of their cottage, and into the long meadow dotted with oak trees.

'Daddy said the lambs are over on the other side of the stream,' Poppy explained to Aunt Violet as they trotted along.

'Stream? Did I hear you say there was a stream, Poppy? We're not going near any water, are we?' Mrs Bottomley snapped.

Aunt Violet turned around. 'There's a bridge, you old fusspot,' she fumed at the teacher. She looked down at Poppy and whispered, 'There is a bridge, isn't there?'

The child nodded. 'Of course.'

Aunt Violet smiled, relieved.

Clementine and Sophie were walking a little further behind.

'What happened to her?' Sophie asked, pointing at Clemmie's great-aunt.

Clementine shrugged. 'I don't know. I think

Grandpa must have told her to be on her best behaviour today.'

'Do you think she'll turn back?' Sophie whispered.

'Into what?' Clementine asked.

'Herself,' Sophie said.

'I hope not. I like her much better this way,' said Clementine.

The children reached the stream where a lovely little stone bridge spanned the banks.

'The sheep are down there,' said Poppy, pointing ahead. Some of the sheep were grazing and others were lying on the grass. In among the mature animals there were lots of lambs.

'Well, have a look, children,' Mrs Bottomley instructed, 'there are the lambs.'

'You can't even see them,' Joshua whined. 'They're too far away.'

'Yes,' Aunt Violet agreed. 'Do you think we can get a little bit closer, Poppy?'

The child nodded. 'Yes, but I don't think we'll be able to touch them.'

'Right, come along then, children,' Aunt

Violet said and began to walk further into the paddock.

'I think we should be getting back soon, Miss Appleby,' Mrs Bottomley declared.

'Nonsense, woman. We've been gone all of fifteen minutes. Unless the Bauers have a supercharged barbecue, those sausages will need a little longer yet.' Aunt Violet shook her head and kept walking.

Clementine and Sophie looked at each other and giggled. It was funny to hear a grown-up talk back to Mrs Bottomley.

Up close, the children could see lots of lambs gambolling about. The little creatures would run quickly past their mothers, as if to show them how steady they were on their feet, then become overwhelmed with shyness and race back for protection.

Poppy warned the group that sometimes the mothers were very bossy and they shouldn't get too close. For the first few minutes everyone had a lovely time watching. Unfortunately that didn't last long.

Joshua had his eye on a tiny lamb. He was determined to catch it and show everyone how clever he was. The boy crept up on the little creature and made a lunge. It skipped out of his grasp and ran towards its mother. Joshua landed on the soft grass, a huge grin on his face.

'Come back here,' he growled, and jumped to his feet.

Mrs Bottomley turned and saw the lad chasing after the lamb. 'Joshua Tribble, stop that at once,' she shouted.

But Mrs Bottomley's shouting only seemed to make the other children excited. Angus took off after another lamb, then Eddie Whipple got in on the act too.

Soon some of the girls joined in the game until sheep, lambs and children scattered over the field like a bag of marbles spilled onto a concrete floor.

Poppy shouted at them to stop. Mrs Bottomley charged through a brambly hedge after Joshua. Aunt Violet had grabbed Angus's collar and was trying to keep a grip on him when Mrs Bottomley began to wail. Clementine and Sophie, who had been standing under one of the oak trees and wondering what was going to happen next, watched wide-eyed as Mrs Bottomley flew out of the hedge with a giant white goose honking and hissing after her.

'Eloise!' Poppy called. 'Leave Mrs Bottomley alone.'

But the goose was not about to stop. Mrs Bottomley wobbled on her feet as she tried to fend off the snapping beak.

'Oh, for heaven's sake, woman. It's a goose, not a charging bull,' chided Aunt Violet. She dropped Angus like a stone and hurried after Mrs Bottomley.

The children all stopped their running about and watched Aunt Violet chasing the goose that was chasing Mrs Bottomley. Joshua began to laugh. Angus did too and soon the whole class was in fits as the two old women and the goose disappeared through the hedge again.

'Where are they?' Angus asked after the trio had been gone a while.

'I'll go and look,' Poppy called.

'I'm coming too,' Angus said.

Astrid's brows knotted together fiercely. 'No, we should all stay here.'

'You're not the boss of us,' Joshua said.

Ella, a tiny girl with long blonde plaits, began to cry. 'Where's Mrs Bottomley?' she sniffled.

Some of the other children were beginning to get upset too. They realised they were alone in the field and the two adults looking after them had vanished.

Poppy grabbed Clementine's hand and together they ran to the edge of the field and scanned the paddock beyond the hedge.

'Where did they go?' Clementine asked as she looked into the empty stretch of green.

'I don't know.' Poppy looked up and down. It seemed the women and the goose had disappeared into thin air.

'What should we do?' Clementine asked.

'We should go and get Daddy,' Poppy declared.

Clementine and Poppy raced back to the oak tree, where the rest of the class was standing.

'Where are they?' Angus asked.

Poppy shrugged.

'I'm going to look,' Joshua declared. 'Because I'm a proper explorer. Girls aren't. They're dumb.'

'We are not,' Clementine said. 'And we're just as good at exploring as you are.'

'Are not,' Joshua spat back.

'We are so,' Clementine shouted at him. She could feel the red rising on her neck.

'Why don't we split up?' Astrid suggested. 'I can take anyone who wants to go back, and Poppy can take anyone who wants to search.'

It sounded reasonable enough to Clementine. She was keen to find Aunt Violet. She didn't think her mummy would be very happy if she lost her, although Uncle Digby probably wouldn't mind.

'Who wants to go with Poppy?' Astrid asked.

Clementine, Sophie, Angus and Joshua put up their hands.

'Who wants to go back?'

A small sea of hands shot into the air.

'I'm starving,' Eddie Whipple groaned.

'Yeah, me too,' said Lester.

'I'll tell your dad where you are, Poppy,' said Astrid. 'Come on then.' She beckoned to the children and began to lead the group back across the field. The sheep and their lambs had all relocated to a quiet spot much further down the paddock.

'Thanks,' Poppy called after her. She turned to the four intrepid adventurers who had stayed behind. 'Now, you have to listen to me because I know everywhere on the farm and I don't want anyone else to get lost.'

'Boring,' Joshua said.

'You can go back with the others if you're going to say that,' Poppy snapped.

'You can't make me,' Joshua said.

'But I will,' Angus growled. He was growing impatient and wanted to find his missing grandmother.

Joshua rolled his eyes.

'We have to stay together,' Poppy said. 'Come on, let's go.'

GONE

A strid led the rest of the children back to the farmhouse, where the smell of barbecued sausages filled the air.

Lily Bauer looked up from where she was cutting bread rolls in half to see the children trooping into the back garden.

'Hello there. What have you done with Mrs Bottomley?' Lily asked.

'She's gone,' Eddie Whipple said.

Lily frowned. 'What do you mean?'

Astrid spoke up. 'Mrs Bottomley and Clementine's great-aunt disappeared.'

'Disappeared?' said Sophie Rousseau's mother anxiously. She was looking around the group of children and noticed that her own daughter and her friends were missing too.

'Well, we went to see the lambs and then Mrs Bottomley got chased by a goose. It was very angry. Then Clementine's great-aunt chased the goose and they all disappeared,' Astrid explained.

Lily Bauer looked at Odette Rousseau in alarm. 'And where's Poppy?'

'And Sophie?' Mrs Rousseau added.

'Poppy said that she knows everywhere on the farm so she's gone to look for them with Sophie and Clementine, and Joshua and Angus too,' said Astrid.

Lily didn't like the sound of this at all. It was bad enough that no one had located Granny Bert yet, but now Mrs Bottomley and Aunt Violet were missing too, and the children had formed a search party. She knew that Poppy was reliable but Angus and Joshua out there could spell trouble.

'Heinrich, I think you should go and find the children,' Lily suggested as her husband lifted the last of the sausages from the barbecue plate. 'We can get lunch organised for this lot.'

Her husband nodded.

Mr Tribble offered to go too, seeing as Joshua was with them.

Meanwhile, out in the field, Poppy decided that they should head towards the edge of the woods, which was the direction they had last seen Mrs Bottomley and Aunt Violet running.

'They can't be too far,' she said as the five children trooped along.

They came to a stone wall. It wasn't especially high but would have presented a challenge for most five-year-olds.

'How are we supposed to get over that?' Sophie asked.

'Me and Angus can do it,' Joshua bragged. 'Because we're commandos.'

'No you're not,' Sophie said. 'You're little boys.'

'It's okay.' Poppy pointed further along. 'There's a stile.'

'I'm going first.' Joshua raced ahead to where the little ladder straddled the wall. He rushed up and then jumped off the other side.

'Pooh!' he yelled.

'What's the matter now?' Poppy asked. She clambered up the ladder and stood on the top rung. Joshua had landed smack bang in the middle of a cow pat.

Sophie scurried up the ladder next. She held her nose and said, 'That's disgusting.' The two girls giggled.

'You're disgusting.' Joshua hissed and pulled a face.

Angus and Clementine joined the others on the far side of the wall and the five children carried on walking.

'Do you really think they could have come this far?' Clementine asked. She noticed that beyond the field there was thick woodland.

'We can go back if you like,' Poppy said. She was surprised that Aunt Violet and Mrs Bottomley hadn't reappeared.

Clementine shook her head. 'I don't want Aunt Violet to be lost.' She never thought she'd say it, but it was true.

IN A FLAP

The goose called Eloise had chased Mrs Bottomley over a wall and deep into the woods. Aunt Violet followed, waving her arms about and yelling at the white bird.

Mrs Bottomley stumbled and fell backwards and the goose seized her opportunity. She leapt onto the woman's chest. Aunt Violet couldn't believe what she was seeing.

Mrs Bottomley flapped her arms at the creature and screamed.

'Good heavens, get off her.' Aunt Violet

pushed against the goose's sizable rump. Eloise turned and snapped at Aunt Violet, who retreated. The creature turned her attention back to Mrs Bottomley.

Eloise thrust her beak forward and grabbed hold of the shiny silver whistle around the teacher's neck. She pulled at the cord.

'It's strangling me,' Mrs Bottomley wailed.

'Give it to her,' said Aunt Violet.

'What?'

'The whistle, woman. She's after the whistle.' Aunt Violet knelt beside Mrs Bottomley's head and pulled the cord from around her neck. She then played tug-of-war with the goose, who still had the whistle firmly in her beak.

'Why, you beastly creature!' Aunt Violet pulled one way and the goose pulled the other. 'Have your way then!'

As soon as Aunt Violet let go of the whistle, the creature turned and waddled off at lightning pace into the woods.

Ethel Bottomley sat up. She exhaled loudly but didn't seem to be able to find any words.

Aunt Violet was similarly dumbstruck.

The two sat in silence for several minutes.

'Well, that was unexpected,' Aunt Violet said, looking distastefully at the brown marks on her white suit.

'I . . . I think you saved my life, Miss Appleby,' Mrs Bottomley stammered.

'Well, I wouldn't go that far,' Aunt Violet replied. 'But you were in a bit of trouble there.'

A tear fell onto Mrs Bottomley's cheek.

'Are you all right?' Aunt Violet offered her hand and pulled the woman to her feet.

'I think it's just all a bit of a shock.' Mrs Bottomley began to cry.

'Come now, Mrs Bottomley,' Aunt Violet soothed.

Without warning, Ethel Bottomley launched herself at Aunt Violet and hugged her tightly. 'Thank you, Miss Appleby. Thank you,' she sobbed.

Violet Appleby stood rigid for a few moments, wondering what she should do. Then she did the only thing possible and hugged Ethel Bottomley right back.

Seconds later, the women separated and Mrs Bottomley sniffed loudly. 'Where are we?' she asked.

'I don't know.' Aunt Violet looked around under the gloomy canopy of trees. Up ahead she spied a stone wall and a stile leading to an open field. 'I think perhaps we should go that way.'

Mrs Bottomley hobbled along beside her and together they somehow managed to get up and over the stile and into the meadow.

Aunt Violet peered into the afternoon sun. 'I think there's a stream down there. Perhaps it's the one we crossed earlier.'

'I don't know if I can walk much further,' Mrs Bottomley whimpered. Her bunions were aching and she had two enormous blisters on her heels.

The ladies ambled on until they reached an enormous fir tree amid a grove of trees. The dappled light danced around its branches, which scooped towards the ground.

Something caught Aunt Violet's eye. She peered through the foliage. 'Goodness me!'

She lifted the branch and disappeared through the other side.

'Please don't leave me behind,' Mrs Bottomley wailed.

'I'm coming back for you.' Aunt Violet held the branch up and Mrs Bottomley followed her.

'What is this place?' Mrs Bottomley said as she looked about. There was an old kitchen cabinet with a sink, a pine dresser full of china and even a chandelier hanging from one of the branches overhead.

Two green armchairs faced away from them, towards a mock fireplace, and there was a round pine table and four chairs set up as if someone was expected for afternoon tea.

'What do you think it is?' Mrs Bottomley whispered. 'You don't think anyone lives here, do you?'

Aunt Violet smiled and shook her head. 'Of course not. It's a cubbyhouse.'

A silver head peered around the side of one of the armchairs. 'Oh, hello there, dears. I've been expecting you.'

Aunt Violet and Mrs Bottomley spun around. 'Who are you?' they asked in unison.

Heinrich Bauer and Mr Tribble set off on foot to locate the children and lost ladies. Mr Greening had telephoned a few minutes before they left to say that there was no sign of Granny Bert in the village either.

'This is not quite the day I had planned,' Heinrich frowned.

'No, but at least it will be one the children will remember,' Mr Tribble replied cheerily. 'Surely they can't be too far. Besides, there's nothing especially dangerous out here, is there?'

Heinrich began to shake his head then stopped. He thought for a moment. 'Well, apart from the geese, perhaps there is something else.'

'What is it?' Mr Tribble asked.

'I forgot about Ramon,' Heinrich replied.

'Who's Ramon?'

Heinrich gulped. 'He's our ram and I'm afraid he's not very fond of children.'

'He's only a sheep. Surely he couldn't do that much damage,' Mr Tribble replied. 'Where is he?'

'He's in the far meadow just this side of the woods. I moved him yesterday, so Poppy would have no idea that he's there. And you're wrong about Ramon. I've seen him flatten three grown men, myself included. Come on, Mr Tribble, we need to get to him before anyone else does.'

The two men jogged into the long meadow and across the stone bridge over the stream. They looked up and down the length of the field and raced towards the far meadow and the woods beyond.

RAMMED

Poppy, Clementine, Sophie and the two boys walked in single file across the far meadow towards the fence.

'What's that?' Joshua looked around just in time to see a huge woolly beast charging towards them.

The other children stopped and looked too.

'Oh my goodness,' Poppy yelled. 'It's Ramon. RUN!'

The children took off as fast as they could. But Ramon was speedy for a sheep. He put his

head down and raced towards them, bleating loudly.

Poppy and Sophie reached the stone wall and scrambled up using the rocks as footholds. Clementine tripped on a stone in the grass and was sent sprawling.

Angus and Joshua were behind her. Joshua kept running but Angus stopped to see if she was all right.

'Come on,' the boy said and grabbed Clemmie's arm.

'My knee hurts,' she whimpered.

Ramon was getting closer and closer.

'Run, Clemmie, run!' Poppy called. Joshua reached the wall and was trying to climb, but his foot kept slipping back.

'Help! He's gonna eat me,' the boy wailed.

Clementine and Angus reached the wall too. Angus scrambled up first and then hauled Clemmie up behind him.

Ramon was flying towards Joshua when all of a sudden the beast pulled up just short of the boy. The ram sniffed. He pawed at the ground and bleated loudly.

'What's he doing?' Angus asked, wondering if he was about to toss Joshua over the wall.

'Joshua, have you got any food in your pockets?' Poppy asked.

Joshua shook his head. Then he remembered he'd stolen an extra brownie at morning tea time. 'Maybe,' he said. He reached into his pocket. 'I've got this.' The brownie was a lot flatter than when he'd shoved it in there.

'Give it to him,' Poppy yelled. 'Hold your hand out flat and give it to him.'

'To the *sheep*?' Joshua asked, frowning.

'Yes, to Ramon. He loves chocolate. As soon as he takes it, climb onto the wall,' the girl replied.

Joshua wondered what sort of sheep ate chocolate. He held out the squished cake and waited. Ramon sniffed his hand then licked his palm.

'That tickles,' the boy giggled.

Ramon began to nibble at the brownie. Then he chewed it for a minute or so before gulping it down. Joshua had just enough time to clamber onto the top of the stone wall.

'Dumb sheep,' Joshua said. 'He's not scary.'

Ramon then charged forward and head-butted the wall with such force that the stones on top shook. Joshua wobbled and just managed to stay upright.

'Yes, he is.' The boy raced along the wall to the stile, where his friends were waiting. 'He could have killed me.'

'Yeah, but he didn't,' Angus replied. He turned to Clementine. 'Your knee's bleeding. Here, have this.' Angus pulled a clean white handkerchief from his pocket and handed it to Clemmie, who mopped up the blood.

'Thank you, Angus,' she said. 'You saved me from that crazy sheep.'

Angus smiled. 'It was nothing.'

'Come on.' Joshua jumped down from the wall. 'Let's go and find those stupid old ladies.'

Angus glared at the boy. Poppy did too.

A VERY STRANGE TEA PARTY

P oppy led the children along the edge of the woods.

'Mrs Bottomley!' Sophie called.

'Aunt Violet, where are you?' Clementine called too.

The children were making as much noise as they possibly could, but there was still no reply.

'I wonder why Mrs Bottomley doesn't just blow her whistle,' Clementine said. 'Then we could find them.'

'I'm hungry,' Joshua grumbled. 'I want my brownie back.'

'You shouldn't have had it in the first place,' Sophie said. 'But it's lucky you did, or you'd probably have a very sore bottom right now.'

The other children giggled.

'Let's go home and see if they've turned up there,' said Poppy. 'I know a shortcut.'

'It better not be anywhere near that sheep again,' warned Joshua.

Poppy shook her head. 'It's not.'

The children all agreed. They had no idea what time it was but it was quite likely the adults would be getting worried about them by now.

They climbed up and over another stile and sped across an open field. Poppy assured everyone that Ramon couldn't get near them, but they decided to go as quickly as they could just to be on the safe side.

The children crossed into the far end of the long meadow.

'Shh, what's that noise?' Clementine said.

'I can't hear anything except the lambs and some ducks,' Sophie replied.

Clemmie listened more closely. 'No, there's something else.'

The children entered a grove of trees. The sound of muffled laughter was unmistakable.

'It's coming from over there,' called Clemmie. She ran towards the giant fir tree.

'That's our cubby,' said Poppy, and chased after her. She pulled back the branch that shielded the entry and the children followed her inside. They couldn't believe their eyes.

'Nan?' Angus exclaimed.

'Aunt Violet, what are you doing here?' Clementine asked.

Poppy's jaw dropped. 'Granny Bert!'

The three elderly women were sitting around the pine kitchen table, laughing like hyenas.

The children noticed the old chipped teacups and saucers on the table. They were completely dry.

Aunt Violet turned and smiled at the group. 'Oh, thank heavens.'

'We're saved!' said Mrs Bottomley, clasping her hands together.

Granny Bert frowned. 'You didn't tell me you'd invited more guests.'

'Granny, it's me, Poppy.' The girl walked over and stood in front of the woman.

'Poppy, of course I know it's you. Do you think I'm losing my marbles?' Granny Bert said with a broad grin.

The children didn't know what to think.

'What are you doing here?' Angus asked.

'We found this place by accident and Mrs Rumble was here already, so we thought we'd just sit and have a rest before we tried to find our way back to the house. I'm afraid your grandmother has some terrible blisters,' Aunt Violet explained.

'But what were you laughing about?' Clementine asked.

'What were we laughing about?' Aunt Violet looked at the other ladies, who shrugged.

'Do we need to have a reason to laugh?' Mrs Bottomley asked. 'I think young people these days take life far too seriously.'

Aunt Violet began to giggle. Granny Bert did too. Mrs Bottomley roared with laughter.

The children didn't understand any of it.

'Are you going to be friends now?' Clementine asked her great-aunt when the laughter finally died down.

'Friends? With Mrs Bottomley? I can't imagine it, dear. She's a dreadful woman,' Aunt Violet said with a grin.

Clementine gasped. 'Aunt Violet, she's sitting right next to you.'

'Yes, I can see her. I don't think she can see me, though. You know she's blind as a bat and deaf as a beetle.'

The other children gasped too.

Mrs Bottomley's eyes crinkled. 'But that's all right, Clementine, because your great-aunt is quite the rudest woman I've ever met in my life and I wouldn't want to be friends with her either.'

The children all gulped and wondered what was about to happen next.

'Oh, for goodness sake, we're joking. We're pulling your legs.' Aunt Violet nudged Mrs Bottomley, who grinned.

'Miss Appleby saved me from that crazy goose. If it wasn't for her, I'd probably be lying in the field with that giant white monster taking a nap on my belly.' The children looked from one woman to the next, wondering what had happened out there. 'But I do think we should be getting back before Mr Bauer does something ridiculous like call the police. Angus, you can wait here with me and I think you should wait here too, Mrs Rumble,' directed Mrs Bottomley. 'Are you right to go with the children, Miss Appleby?'

Violet Appleby stood up. 'Yes, of course.'

Granny Bert nodded. 'I don't know where Lily got to with that morning tea, but I wish she'd hurry up.'

'Come along, Clementine,' Aunt Violet instructed.

Clemmie walked towards her great-aunt. The woman slipped her hand into Clemmie's and they followed Poppy, Sophie and Joshua out of the cubby.

'There's Daddy,' Poppy shouted. She began to race towards the figure in the distance.

'Aunt Violet, are you really going to be friends with Mrs Bottomley?' Clementine looked up at the woman. Aunt Violet's hair was rumpled and her white suit was a patchwork of brown and green stains.

Aunt Violet smiled. 'Let's just say that sometimes it takes a fiasco to help two stubborn old women understand one another.'

'What's a fiasco?' Clementine had never heard that word before.

'A disaster,' her great-aunt replied. 'And I think today has been just that, don't you?'

Clementine shook her head. 'No, Aunt Violet, I don't think so at all. Angus saved me from Ramon and Joshua saved himself with a chocolate brownie and you saved Mrs Bottomley and made a new friend. So I'd say that today has been just about perfect. Wouldn't you?'

Aunt Violet smoothed her hair and then grinned. 'Perhaps. But you're not to breathe a word of any of this to Pertwhistle or your mother. Do you understand?'

Clementine nodded. Maybe she didn't mind having a secret with Aunt Violet after all.

ANOTHER SECRET

E veryone was relieved when Aunt Violet appeared with the children. Mr Bauer had raced home to get the four-wheel drive and transport Mrs Bottomley and Granny Bert back to the farmhouse. Lily found some bandaids for Mrs Bottomley's blisters and insisted that the woman sit in the garden to rest.

Although lunch was late for some, it was delicious and much appreciated. After everyone had eaten, Aunt Violet took charge and the children had a wonderful time identifying and pulling up some vegetables, and meeting a couple of the horses which Max, the stablehand at Highton Hall, brought down especially.

'I think it's almost time to go,' said Aunt Violet. She could hear the rattle of the bus coming down the lane. 'Gather up your bags children and let's go and meet Mr Stubbs, shall we?'

Mrs Bottomley appeared and insisted that everyone line up so she could call the roll.

Aunt Violet let her go. It was still her excursion after all, and at least she no longer had that dreadful whistle.

'Where's Joshua Tribble?' Mrs Bottomley asked, looking straight at the boy's father.

'He's just gone to the toilet,' Mr Tribble replied.

'Well, go and get him,' Mrs Bottomley demanded. 'We need to get moving.' Mrs Bottomley had had quite enough adventures for one day – and although it was tempting to leave the boy behind, she could only imagine what Miss Critchley would have to say about that.

'Good day, Ethel?' Bernie Stubbs asked as Mrs Bottomley boarded the bus.

'Yes, Mr Stubbs. A surprisingly good day,' the woman replied.

He grinned. 'I do like to hear that.'

The children bade farewell to Mr and Mrs Bauer, Poppy and Granny Bert, and thanked them loudly for a wonderful day.

'So what do you think of life on a farm?' Mr Tribble asked his son as they sat together in the middle of the bus.

'It's okay,' said Joshua. 'But I don't like sheep much.'

Clementine was sitting in the front seat next to Aunt Violet. As the bus lurched forward, bumping along the narrow country lane, she was surprised to see Eloise the goose waddling between two of the sheds with what looked like Mrs Bottomley's shiny silver whistle around her neck.

She turned to her great-aunt. 'Did you see that?'

Aunt Violet raised her eyebrows and smiled. 'Let's just hope she doesn't learn how to use it. Can I tell you a secret, Clementine?'

Clementine looked at her great-aunt cautiously. She already had the secret of the crystal vase to worry about, and not telling about today's adventure with Mrs Bottomley and Eloise. 'Okay.'

The old woman whispered, 'I think I actually enjoyed myself at the farm. It was a most unpredictable outing.'

Clementine looked at her in shock. 'That's the secret?'

Aunt Violet nodded.

Clementine leaned in and cuddled her. 'Thank you, Aunt Violet.'

'Whatever for?' her great-aunt asked.

Clementine grinned. 'For being unpredictable too.'

CAST OF CHARACTERS

The Appleby household

Clementine Rose Appleby	Five-year-old daughter of Lady Clarissa
Lavender	Clemmie's teacup pig
Lady Clarissa Appleby	Clementine's mother and the owner of Penberthy House
Digby Pertwhistle	Butler at Penberthy House
Aunt Violet Appleby	Clementine's grandfather's sister
Pharaoh	Aunt Violet's beloved sphynx cat

School staff and students

Miss Arabella Critchley	Head teacher at Ellery Prep
Mrs Ethel Bottomley	Teacher at Ellery Prep
Sophie Rousseau	Clementine's best friend – also five years old
Poppy Bauer	Clementine's good friend – also five years old
Angus Archibald	Kindergarten boy
Joshua Tribble	Naughty friend of Angus's
Astrid	Clever kindergarten girl
Eddie Whipple, Lester, Ella	Kindergarten classmates

Others

Odette Rousseau	Sophie's mother
Mr Tribble	Joshua's father
Heinrich Bauer	Poppy's father, manages the farm at Highton Hall
Lily Bauer	Poppy's mother, works on the farm and at Highton Hall

Granny Bert (Albertine Rumble)	Elderly lady, lives next to the farm in Rose Cottage
Daisy Rumble	Granny Bert's granddaughter, also lives at Rose Cottage
Bernie Stubbs	Bus driver

ABOUT THE AUTHOR

Jacqueline Harvey taught for many years in girls' boarding schools. She is the author of the bestselling Alice-Miranda series and the Clementine Rose series, and was awarded Honour Book in the 2006 Australian CBC Awards for her picture book *The Sound of the Sea*. She now writes full-time and is working on more Alice-Miranda and Clementine Rose adventures.

www.jacquelineharvey.com.au

Look out for Clementine Rose's next adventure

CLEMENTINE ROSE

and the Seaside Escape

March 2014

Collect the series

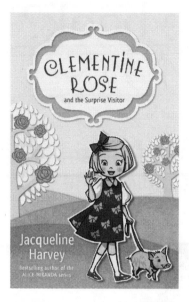

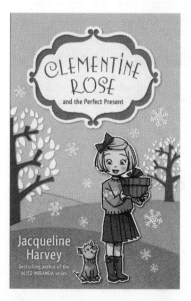

Loved the book?

There's so much more
stuff to check out online

AUSTRALIAN READERS:

randomhouse.com.au/kids

NEW ZEALAND READERS:

randomhouse.co.nz/kids